Dead Inside

Yaadon Ki Pustak

Shubh Srivastava

ISBN 978-93-5458-203-5
© Shubh Srivastava 2021
Published in India 2021 by Pencil

A brand of
One Point Six Technologies Pvt. Ltd.
123, Building J2, Shram Seva Premises,
Wadala Truck Terminal, Wadala (E)
Mumbai 400037, Maharashtra, INDIA
E connect@thepencilapp.com
W www.thepencilapp.com

DISCLAIMER: *The opinions expressed in this book are those of the authors and do not purport to reflect the views of the Publisher.*

Author biography

Shubh Srivastava is an aspiring writer. He is currently pursuing Bachelor of Technology from Awadh University. During his dark phase of life, he wrote poetry to express his feelings. Now that he is out of it he wants to share with the world, his untouched feelings.

CONTENTS

Epigraph

The words are souls of language & often misunderstanding of other's speech will create communication gap , becomes the reason for breaking relation. Abstract languages like painting / mathematics / poetry etc binds thousands of truth effectively by various forms like image / Sutra's (Formula) / metaphor. Expressing thought with minimum worlds immensely helps us. It saves time. Concise, precise clear speaking will not be possible if progress in linguistic word, languages is stopped. In short, enrichment of language, art has contribution in enrichment of society. So it is essential to understand abstract language , it's soul i.e. words & give support / encouragement to ongoing research in such field by acknowledging / participating in it. We need to invent new form to express thought clearly. In this book. I had taken little bit effort to bring few new form of poetry. The book shows the beauty of Hindi words. Book is useful for all Hindi Professor, poetry lovers

& almost all. Artist / producer / leader & almost all of us needs effective words, metaphor, forms to express our thought, deliver speech effectively. Not only thought should be noble but it is equally important to express it in the attractive form. The book tries to experiment with Hindi words. One can also extend the approach for other languages.

Foreword

Hindi was never my preffered language to write in. I always found it very difficult to write in hindi but when you are feeling low and don't have the courage or strength to share your hurtful feelings with anyone, be it your closest friend or family member, you turn to words. They give you the love and support you so dearly need. They provide you with warmth and kindness, they listen to your unspoken words. The same happened with me. I turned to words both english and hindi. So ahead are some of the poems that i wrote in hindi while battling depression. They are not as perfect as the english ones but i tried my best to deliver my heartfelt emotions using the quickest words that got into my mind. so please forgive me for my mistakes.

I hope you will enjoy it.

Introduction

To all the readers, In the upcoming pages you will find my battle of depression through poetry exclusively written through that period. Hope you relate to it and give the book some love. To everyone who is battling depression or any other mental health problems you have my love and support. Fight the darkness and there will be light. Thank you.

vo...

वो सुबह ही क्या
जो गमगीन ना हो,
वो शाम ही क्या
जो रानगीन ना हो,
और ग़ालिब;
वो रात ही क्या जो
ढलने को मजबूर ना हो।

Main...

मै बैठा रहा उनके इंतज़ार में
एक इन्तहां हो गयी उनके प्यार में
वो आयी न कभी मेरे सामने
बस मिलने क ख्वाब दिखाती रही घने

Malaal...

चूड़ियां खनक रही थी
मंत्र गूंज रहे थे
खुशमुमा माहोल था
मैफिल-ए-जाम था
बस मलाल इस बात का था
की उसके साथ कोई और था
और मैं बस एक अनजान था

Kalam....

उनके जज़्बातों की धार को
मैंने अपनी कलम में पिरोया
पर जब कागज़ पर उतरा
तो ज़लज़ला नज़र आया

Yaari....

बरसों की यारी
साथ खेलना
साथ खाना
थोड़ा लड़ना
थोड़ा झगड़ना
फिर मनान
ओर मस्ती में रुलना
साथ बड़ना
साथ उडना
साथ रेहना
आज छूट रही है वो यारी
मुझे दूर जा रहे वो यारी
मेरा वो भाई
जिसने कभी डांट ना लगाई
मेरी वो बेहेन
जिसने कभी आँख न दिखाई
मेरी वो प्यरी
जो थी सब पे भारी
आज जा रही वो यारी
जने कब मिलेंगे फिर

कब होंगी वो मुलाकतें
जीनमे थी बरसों की बातें
आज जा रही वो यात्रि

Ghar ki yaad.....

हालात वही हैं
पर जज़्बात अलग हैं
रास्ता वही है
पर बात अलग है
रात वही है
पर नींद अलग है

Doobta suraj....

डूबते सूरज सी है जिंदगी
प्यारी तो है पर हमारी नहीं
सुन्दर तो है पर मुक्कदर नहीं ।

उसे मालूम है उसे डूबना होगा
चांद के वास्ते उसे मरना होगा
पर खूबसूरती है उन आंखों में अभी
मरना है जिन्हे अप्र हाथों ही कभी ।

Mohabbat aur Ashiqui....

समुंदर के किनारे भी मुझे पानी ना मिला
बवंडर के अंदर भी मुझे बयार ना मिली।
जाने किस रास्ते पे चला हूं मैं
ना मोहब्बत मिली ना आशिकी ही मिली।

shayar....

एक शायर को लिखने के लिए दुख की जरुरत नही होती
वो रोशिनी को भी राख में बदल अपने पन्नों में पिरो लेता हैं

Dhadkan...

मैं अक्सर सोचता हूँ कि क्या धड़कन थकती नहीं
वो क्यूँ चलती ही जाती है,
चलती ही जाती है
क्या वो किसी की खोज मे है?
कोई अपना .....जो बरसों पहले खो गया हो
या क्या वो किसी से भाग रही है?
जैसे कोई उसके पीछे पड़ा हो।

जाने क्यूँ चल रही है
एक पल को रुक क्यूँ नही जाती,
एक पल को थम क्यूँ नही जाती,
एक पल को सुकून से.... सो क्यूँ नही जाती।

मैं इंतज़ार में हूँ उस लम्हे के
मैं बेकरार हूँ उसके थमने के
क्योंकि थक मैं भी गया हूँ
उसे रोज भागता देख
उसे रोज़ मरता देख.....

Yaadein.....

कही गुम सी गई हैं वो यादें
जिनमें थे बरसों के वादे

कही खो सी गई है वो मुस्कान
जो मिटाती थी सबकी रुझान

कुछ भूल से गए हैं वो सपनें
जिनमें थे हजारों अपने

आज खुले आसमान तले बैठा हूँ मैं
सितारों के संग भी अकेला हूँ मैं

उस उजाले की तलाश में हूँ
जब अन्धकार के पास मैं हूँ

जाने कब आएंगी वो घडियां
जिनमें होंगी खुशिओं की फुलझड़ियां ।

ABOUT DEPRESSION

Before we begin reding my poetry, it is important that we understand what depression really is. So let us read about it and educate ourselves about it in this chapter after which my raw feelings in the form of poetry will begin. So here we go,

Depression refers to a medical disorder that leads to feelings of loss of interest, as well as feelings of sadness. Depression has an impact on how a person behaves, thinks, and feels. There are many physical and emotional problems, which may emanate from depression. Most people suffering from depression may have negative feelings towards themselves. Depression has an impact on the day-to-day activities of an individual, especially during the days when one suffers from depression. Depression is a common illness, and it can have serious implications on a person's life.

Causes of Depression

The causes of depression include a combination of environmental, biological, psychological, as well as genetic factors. When a person is undergoing depression, neurotransmitters tend to be out of balance. Depression is caused by an imbalance in the

various parts of the brain, which control sleep, thinking, behavior, mood, as well as appetite. Depression can also be a genetic disorder that runs in families. Some genes may predispose people to depression, especially when genetic factors combine with environmental factors that cause depression. Other causes of depression include trauma, which may result from losing loved ones, stressful situations, or experiencing difficulty in relationships. There tends to be higher rates of depression in women than in men. This emanates from factors such as psychological factors, hormonal, lifecycle, as well as biological factors, which women tend to experience more than men. For instance, there is a possibility that women will develop postpartum depression upon giving birth, especially because there are some hormonal changes that have taken place and there is the responsibility of taking care of the newborn child.

Depression may also emanate from financial troubles; for example, when a person faces difficulties in raising the money that he or she needs to settle some of his bills. The daily hassles at work can also cause depression. This results from work overload and lack of adequate rest. Conflict with friends and family members can also cause depression. Persistent disputes have been identified as significant causes of depression since they disrupt a person's hormonal balance, as well as how the person thinks. Depression can also be caused by certain medications and drugs that a person could be taking. For instance, drugs used in the treatment of high blood pressure increase the risk of having depression.

Major life events have also been identified as main causes of depression. These events may include been involved in an accident, losing a job, retiring, or going through the rigorous process of divorce. Substance abuse can also cause depression; persons

having substance abuse problems have are vulnerable to either clinical or major depression. Depression can also be caused by personal problems like social isolation, which results from mental illnesses or being left out of social groups or out of the family. Feelings of isolation and loneliness can cause depression since a person may feel not part of the entire society.

SHOULD I CALL IT A NIGHT

Should i call it a night?
Or continue to fight,

For it's been so long
Since I've seen the dawn,

For I've seen the light,
Despise me for my plight,

For it wasn't my fault
Not being the default,

For I've been so down
That the earth may frown,

For the life i live
For the death i wish,

Should I call it a night?
And give up the fight?

WHY

Why was i cursed
With a life on earth
Why was i blessed
With a life so clashed
Why was i born
For the chaos
And to be torn?

NIGHT

It feels right
During night
But it frights
During daylight.

I don't know why
I feel surprised
When I'm living
With a knife
Of ice
Through my eyes.

I feel bad for my thighs
For the pain they feel for nights
Looking for the oasis
Down in the desert of life.

MY...

My head hurts,
My chest burns,
My stomach churns,
My hands search,
for the lost peace,
in the deep seas.

I'd love to breathe,
One last seethe.
I'd love to believe,
that i can still be retrieved.
But I'm dying a death so naive,
when i wanna live a life to perceive.

The sun's setting down,
and the moon's coming around,
And i know I'm gonna drown,
in the grief I renown.

ALIVE IN A MORGUE

I feel trapped
I feel wrapped
In a world that doesn't give a crap
It couldn't be
But really
It's just the people around me
I feel left
In a world of theft
I feel caught
In the net of overwhelming distraught
I feel lost
But every help want's a cost
I feel dead
But i see the people around me mend
Why not me?
And why me?
Is the questions i ask
But people always tend to put on a mask
I put on one too
The mask to hide the taboo

When i should be celebrating it with a woohoo
But i can't do it in true
Because I'm locked alive in a morgue

DEAMON

In the day it's so bright
But when comes the night
And it gets so quiet
A demon comes by
To listen the dreary cries
From the ones that smile
During the day's aisle
Form the ones that try
To correct their sinful lie

He's feared by everyone
And loved by no one
He knows he frightens
When he could provide happiness
But no one believes
What he wants to conceive

He's alone in the night
Waiting for his silver knight
Who'll listen to his cries

Which he lets out every morning when he dies.

LIFE IS PAIN

Life is pain
Where you sometimes gain
But always refrain
From the sad train
But it's a journey you must take
In order reach and overtake
In order to reach
The mountain peak
In order to speak
The loudest speech

Life is pain
But it's also a game
Where you get one life
To make a highscore
Or drown on the shore.

LOVING WHIRL

There once was a girl
Who was in the pool of loving whirl
Pretty it seemed
But violent it deemed
She fought it hard
To be with the love of her cards
She struggled
It fluttered
She fought
It distraught
She stopped to take a breath
And dive into the whirl's depth
She gave it herself
And lay there motionless
When a swirl took her in her arms
And she was far from harm
She took a deep dive
And felt so alive.

BLOOD FROM MY VEINS

Blood from my veins
Flowing onto the floor
I sliced open the door
To heaven's hole
I felt no pain
But a happy grain
I don't fear death
I'm just afraid that I'll be back to health
I cannot not die
Or the cut won't suffice
I want to succumb
And be torn to crumbs.

WHY AM I....

Why am i breathing
When there's no air
Why am i crying
When there's no pain
Why am i smiling
When there's no gain
Why am i walking
Without any place
Why don't i stop it
And end it again
Why am i living
When I'm tired of trying
Why don't i lay down
And get a good night's sleep
Which will last forever
And I'll be happy like a lover.

BEREFT

I walked into a room full of people
But she was the only one i could see
A million other noises
But her's seemed like a melody
My eyes were fixated
On the most beautiful creature
God ever created
I asked her out
She put me down
So i never left
The boat of bereft

THE CLOCK

I'm looking at the clock
It covers all blocks
It never even stops
And gives people hopes
The hopes of life
The hopes of time
The hopes that all wil be fine
When the clock will strike nine
It never gets tired
But is never admired
It's always expected to write
And bring out the bright
But all it can do is hover all night
It only shows the time
But is always on everyone's mind
It represents your life
The time you got left to write
The time you got left to suffice
A life you so dearly despise.

FIGHT

The chirping of the birds,
makes me want to sing a song.
The whispering of the wind,
makes me want to spill all my secrets.
The bright morning light,
makes me want to reach the heights.
But the dark circles under me eyes,
from the long restless nights,
makes me want to lay quite
And end my fight.

THE THIRD DEGREE

She looked in her eyes
The blacked lie
Given to her by the love of her life
And yet she felt pain of a thousand knives

She blemished her bruised
Dressed up as a princess
Put on those heels
And walked down to live the life of reels

She smiled throughout
But never felt proud
She was held softly
That she felt quiverly

She felt like staying
But she knew she needed to leave
For her husband would kill
If she would not bill

She put on a smile
And left the aisle
Tears broke free
As she was on her way to the third degree.

She hid all her pain
To the level where se rained
She put on her mascara
And smiled like a Rivera

THERE WERE NEVER BUTTERFLIES
BUT FIRE

I was on my way with frustration
When she caught me off station
Held my hands tightly
That i could feel the blood in her veins running
fastly
She cuffed my hands behind me
And slammed onto a tree
I could see her rage filled eyes
And it felt like i got a surprise
She had a badge of cop
And i started getting mesmerized by her nonstop
She put me in a van
And gave me a glaring scan
She saw me as her enemy
But it made me full of serenity
I looked into her eye
With a loving vibe
She slapped me across the face
Started questioning me at light's pace

But all i could see
Was her luscious lips
I grabbed her by the hips
And kissed her like time of six
She tried to push me away
But eventually gave herself away
Another cop came
With a warrant of someone else's name
She glared into my eyes
With her sorry arise
But it pierced into my heart
Like a piece of art
She freed my hands
While her pupils expand

She looked into my eyes
Like a warm piece of ice
I took her hands in mine
And wrote my number with shine
She smiled like a seal
That it almost felt surreal.

WISH

Oh how pretty they are
The shoes of the lady with a car
I wish i could travel so far
To be able to buy the star

Oh how delicious that is
The smell of those roasted peas
I wish i could earn with ease
To be able to eat whatever i please

Oh how beautiful that looks
The house on the side of the brooks
I wish i could not have to crook
To be able to have a house to betook

I wish i was rich
As the man on the beach
I wish i live
The life of a fish.

THE STORY OF

It was a hot summer day
When a child was born around hay
Beautiful as she was
Ugly was what lay past
As time got wide
She cried from inside
Oh lord! Oh lord!
Why did you take my best chord?
Why did you put me in the wrong hoard?
Why did you curse me with the worst cure?
Why did you make me coarse instead of pure?
There came no reply
She didn't know why?
Soon she realised
The importance of her life
After failing the death nose dive
She recognised herself for who she was
Not just a body but the soul that crawls
To run out of the body
And find a suitable antibody

She looked at herself and called herself He
He suffered
His existence buffered
But he continued to struggle
To eliminate the trouble

Finally came on day
When he found his bay
Together he was
With his soul without bars.

I LIKE THE NIGHT

I like the night
It's so dark yet so bright
It bring me to light
World's mischievous heights

I like the night
For it's accepts the quiet
And allows them to speak
In the loudest squeak

I like the night
For it lets me cry
And drain my eye
For it hugs me tight
And becomes my knight.
For it helps me write
The world of my plight.

DO I NEED TO WAKE UPD

Do i need to wake up?
And turn the lights up?

When I've befriended the darkness,
Knowing it's a strangling harness;
When the world turned me down,
I took the road to the murky town;
When i felt like a dime,
Amongst the towering pines;
It took me in it's arms,
Like a seedling in the farm;
I know it's clenching my lungs so tight,
But i need it to survive the dreary plight;
For it helps me heal,
From the pains of the teal.

Do i need to wake up?
And turn the lights up?

When I'm smitten by the night,

And despised by the bright.

THE WEAK OF HEART

The weak of the heart they said
But the strong of will they forgot

He walked the knife with a heavy heart;
Ready to end it for once and all.

For peace he thrived;
For love he strived.

He ringed those bells;
Let out some yells.

But 'em ears went deaf;
In hurting they left.

He smiled all along;
Until he couldn't carry on.

Tired of it all;
Death was his only call.

Slipped the knife;
Took the last breath of life.

Gave up the fight;
And fell into the light.

His body ceased;
To find its peace.

They called him a coward
and a weak of heart
When all they did was watch his life
tear itself apart.

DEATH IS;

Death is;
Where you sleep in a case,
And live at the space's pace.

Where you are at the top of a pine,
And at the core of a shrine.

Where you smile through your tears,
And laugh through your fears.

Where you feel the joy like a toy,
You never felt when ahoy .

Where you see the undead ,
And warn them for what lies ahead.

Death is;
What everyone sees,
But no one believes,
Until is restricts your reach,

And your world is breached,
By the unexpected feat.

COERCED HEART

As precious as she was,
coerced was her heart.
She was with me through elation,
but bailed through the misery.
She left me in my darkest days,
when all i needed was the touch of her hands.

DARK ALLEYWAYS

Have you ever seen the sun,
it looks so bright and fun.
My soul burns like it everyday,
still i cannot light up my dark alleyway

MAD GUY

Curious mind now turned into blank space
Bubbly heart now beating at slowest pace
Bad thoughts creeping into my mind
Sad mood hovering all the time

So I'm a sad guy
I like it really bad guy
I'm a mad guy
Looking for death guy
Make my mama sad type
No girlfriend to seduce type
Make furious my dad type
I'm the maaaadd guuuyyy, duh

I'm the mad guy.

WISHFUL BIRD

I was like a desert
When she came in like a wishful bird.
She changed my life forever
And turned the forbidden land
Into a field of beautiful clovers.

MONSTER

Depression is a monster
That destroys both heart and soul.
It tortures without mercy
And consumes its victim whole

DEMONS OF DARKNESS

She stood on the bridge
In silence and fear,
For the demons of darkness
Had driven her here.

They cut her heart
Right out of her chest,
Making her believe
That the demons knew best.

They were always there,
Sometimes just out of sight,
Waiting in the background
Till the time was right.

These demons were destructive,
Knocking down the life she knew,
Hating everything about her;

She hated herself, too.

These demons can't be seen,
But they're far from fairy tales.
They live inside your mind;
Their evilness prevails.

So on the bridge she stood,
About to end the fight.
Then she stopped and thought
I'll fight them one more night.

ONCE, IN MY EARLY THIRTIES...

Once, in my early thirties, I saw
that I was a speck of light in the great
river of light that undulates through time

I was floating with the whole
human family. We were all colors — those
who are living now, those who have died,
those who are not yet born. For a few
moments I floated, completely calm,
and I no longer hated having to exist

Like a crow who smells hot blood
you came flying to pull me out
of the glowing stream.
"I'll hold you up. I never let my dear
ones drown!" After that, I wept for days

THE RAINN...

The rain drums down like red ants,
each bouncing off my window.
The ants are in great pain
and they cry out as they hit
as if their little legs were only
stitched on and their heads pasted.
And oh they bring to mind the grave,
so humble, so willing to be beat upon
with its awful lettering and
the body lying underneath
without an umbrella.
Depression is boring, I think

and I would do better to make
some soup and light up the cave

LATE INTO THE NIGHT

So, we'll go no more a roving
So late into the night,
Though the heart be still as loving,
And the moon be still as bright.
For the sword outwears its sheath,
And the soul wears out the breast,
And the heart must pause to breathe,
And love itself have rest.
Though the night was made for loving,
And the day returns too soon,
Yet we'll go no more a roving
By the light of the moon.